Find Phoebe online at www.phoebethefly.com.

Friend Phoebe at Facebook.com/FlyPhoebeFly

Fly Phoebe Fly!

A Mostly True Story

For Cooper,
I hope this
book inspires
you!

Mike Quinn
2016

By Mike Quinn

Flyco Publishing
We make kids smarter the old fashioned way...
One page at a time!

———

Published by Flyco Publishing
www.flycopublishing.com

Cover, Layout, and Story Peripherals by
Trisha Keel, PhD   Tomorrow's Key

Manufactured in the United States of America

1   3   5   7   9   10   8   6   4   2

Mike Quinn
Fly Phoebe Fly!

———

ISBN-13:978-1530583171
ISBN-10: 1530583179

This book is dedicated to my dad,
William J. Quinn

The Greatest Storyteller Who Ever Lived
April 18, 1934—January 6,2014

Foreward

Phoebe is just like all youngsters. She is curious. She loves to explore. And she loves discovering the wonders of the world. You are invited to join Phoebe as she explores. While Phoebe flies around the world, you will tap into the treasures of the world wide web.

Each page has a sky blue box entitled **Join the Adventure!** Here you will find questions to consider that will enrich and expand your learning. Some questions are easy. Some questions want to know your feelings. Some questions may be answered differently by other people. You decide which answer is right for you. Some questions challenge you to go online or use your computer to find answers.

There is no answer key in this book. Just like Phoebe, if you want to learn, you'll find your way to the answers you seek. Not all questions have a single answer. You may find some questions lead you to more questions. The more you explore and learn, the wiser you will be.

There are lots of links for you to follow. Some are for learning and some are for fun. Words that are written in green are included in the Glossary and Pronunciation Guide in case you have never seen or heard them before. Follow Phoebe's path on the map. Explore a bit more in Fun Facts. Be as worldly as Phoebe and speak FIVE languages with the chart on page 79.

You are invited to visit Phoebe on her website, **www.flyphoebefly.com** to discover what she has been up to lately. She has been talking about sponsoring Phoebe Fairs to encourage kids like you to follow your questions all the way to your answers. Friend Phoebe on Facebook at **www.Facebook.com/FlyPhoebeFly**. You never know where you will find Phoebe next! Write to Phoebe to share your learning adventures at **phoebe@flyphoebefly.com**.

Table of Contents

1

Phoebe Phyllis McGillicutty was born of humble beginnings, in a green plastic trash can in Santa Fe, Texas on a quiet street two miles from town.

The McGillicuttys were a middle class fly family. The food scraps they had were average. Their can was nice, but it wasn't like the shiny metal can the neighbors had. The McGillicutty family had never even tasted lobster or caviar like the Smith family had.

Her mom and dad always said they should all be grateful for what they had.

Join the Adventure!

How can you get to Santa Fe, Texas?

Do you think a green can can be as nice as a shiny metal can?

Have a food adventure and try something you have never eaten before.

What are you grateful for?

Phoebe was the smallest of all her 150 brothers and sisters. Needless to say she got teased a lot.

Her dad used to always say she was the smallest because she was "born on the bony side of the pork chop."

Join the Adventure!

What is teasing?

What did Phoebe's dad mean?

Do Venus Fly Traps really eat flies?

To see how Blue Bottle flies like Phoebe benefit the environment, watch this YouTube video: http://bit.ly/22IPXif

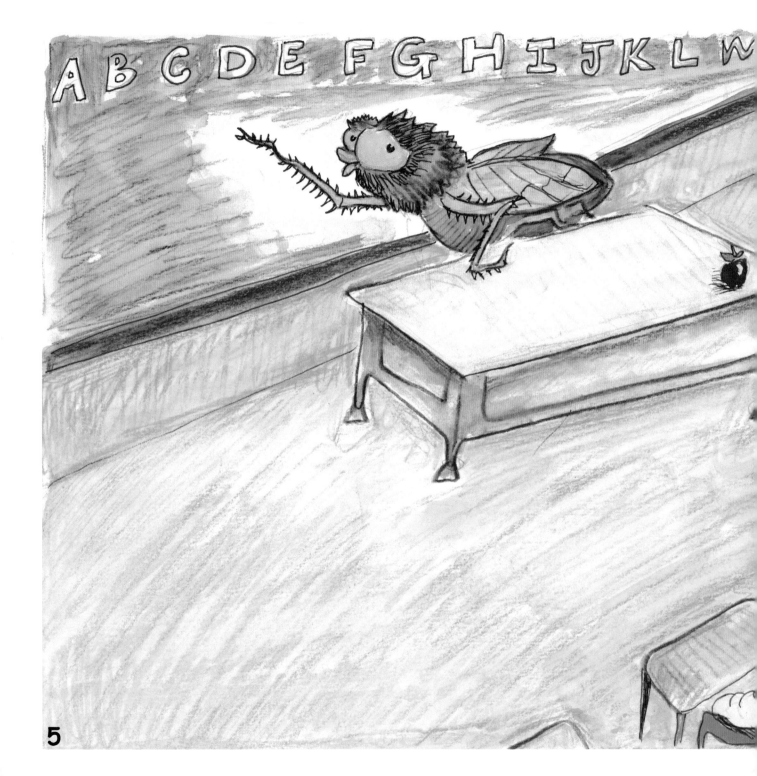

Her mom was well-educated. She was born in a dumpster on the campus of Harvard University. She would always tell them that even though they were common house flies, that shouldn't mean that they live a common life.

Phoebe's mom encouraged all her kids to read. They were all required to read at least one paragraph per day.

Join the Adventure!

Where is Harvard University?

What is a dumpster?

What things do you do to live an uncommon or extraordinary life?

How many paragraphs are on this page?

6

Being small had big advantages. Phoebe could squeeze between all the pages of trash in the can. There were newspapers, magazines, catalogs, and tuna cans.

Phoebe had a knack for reading and had read every scrap of paper in the can in two weeks. She had memorized her address and could recite the credit card numbers from three different cards.

Whenever she wasn't reading, Phoebe was sleeping, dreaming of all the places that she would go.

Join the Adventure!

What is an advantage?

How does tuna get in a can?

What is a catalog?

What is a knack?
What do you have a knack for?

Have you memorized your address?

7

8

Trash day finally arrived. Every member of the McGillicutty family was very excited when they heard the trash truck rumbling down the road.

Phoebe was ready and was the first fly out as the lid swung open. As she flew away, she could hear her mom's encouraging words: "Fly, Phoebe, Fly!"

She flew quickly into the window of the giant truck and settled in behind the driver's seat.

Join the Adventure!

What day is trash day at your home?

Does your family recycle?

Why was the McGillicutty family excited?

How many days does it take for a maggot to turn into a fly?

10

After a grand tour of the whole town the truck stopped.

The trash truck's hydraulics groaned and creaked as the day's collection of trash rolled out onto the base of a huge pile of wondrous garbage.

Phoebe flew out to survey all the new sights and smells. She quickly made her way to the very top of the pile.

In the distance she could see an airport, something she had only read about. Huge flying machines! She left to investigate.

Join the Adventure!

Why do garbage trucks have hydraulics?

Where is your garbage dump located?

What is the difference between garbage and trash?

Why would Phoebe investigate?

Once inside the airport, Phoebe got to try steaming hot pizza for the first time, and even a cold Dr. Pepper®. The hot pizza burned her feet and she cooled them off in a drop of soda.

Join the Adventure!

How could Phoebe get into the airport since she's too little to open a door?

How hot is a pizza oven?

Have you ever had a cold Dr. Pepper®?

How many feet does a fly have?

What is the best first aid for a burn?

The smell of fresh baked bread drew
Phoebe down a narrow hallway. Just as she
flew through the door, it closed behind her.

She was aboard the A-380, the largest
passenger plane in the world!

Join the Adventure!

What smells
better to you than
bread baking?

What is a
jetbridge?

How many people can an
A-380 carry?

How far can a fly fly?

How far can an A-380 fly?

15

Phoebe decided the first class section was more comfortable, and there were far fewer people.

The flight attendant got up and gave a safety demonstration in several different languages.

Join the Adventure!

To see the inside of an A-380 passenger plane, watch this YouTube video: http://bit.ly/1o9Bj3O

What is different between the first class section and the regular section of an airplane?

What is this woman wearing over her shoulders? Why is she wearing it?

Wearing a seat belt was out of the question, so Phoebe hid under the seat of a woman who had a small dog in a carrier.

The dog seemed nervous, but not Phoebe. She flew all the time.

After the plane took off, the lights were turned down and most everyone went to sleep, even the dog.

Twelve hours later the lights came back on, and they were served breakfast. Phoebe feasted on an omelet and toast as the woman tended to her dog.

Join the Adventure!

Why can't Phoebe wear a seatbelt?

Why isn't Phoebe nervous?

Why do people sleep on an airplane?

Is it OK to eat food after a fly has eaten some of it? Why?

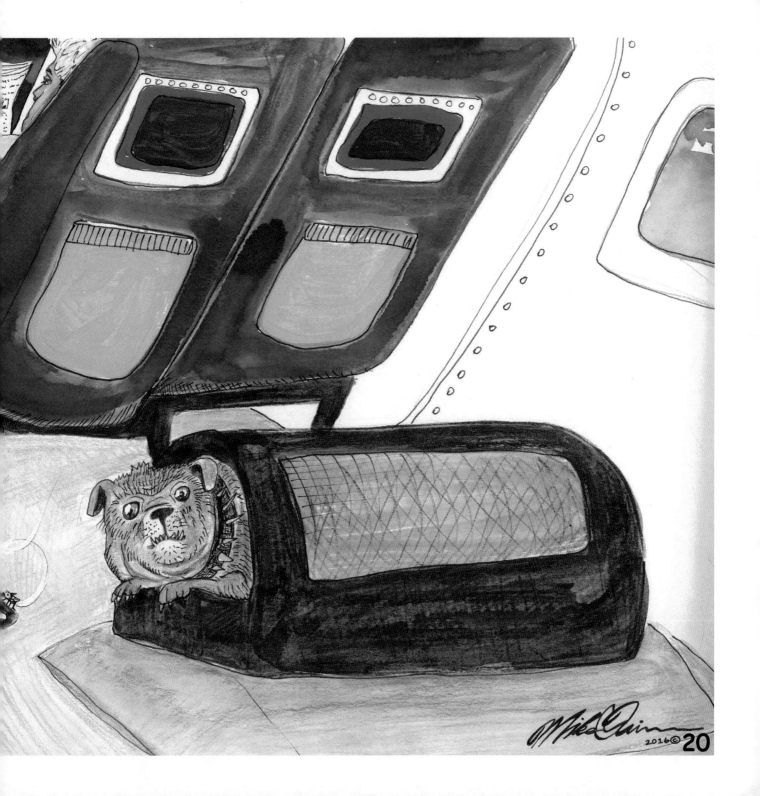

21

The plane finally came to a stop and Phoebe was the first one off the plane.

She breezed right through Customs. It was a good thing she was small, because Phoebe had never even seen a passport before.

She had made it to France. A place she had only read and dreamed about!

Join the Adventure!

How could Phoebe be the first one off the plane?

What is a passport?

How could Phoebe tell she was in France?

How far is France from your home?

Who is the man in blue? How do you know?

She toured the Louvre...

Join the Adventure!

What might you see at the Louvre? Watch this YouTube video http://bit.ly/PhoebeLouvre

Picasso and DaVinci were both artists but painted pictures differently. Why is it important to see things differently?

What is inspiration?

Go to your museum with a tablet and pencil and draw something you see while you are there.

...and visited the Eiffel Tower.

Join the Adventure!

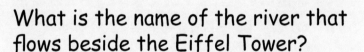

How tall is the tallest place in your town?

How tall is the Eiffel Tower?

What is the name of the river that flows beside the Eiffel Tower?

Why is the bottom of the tower wider than the top?

You can take a virtual tour of the Eiffel Tower at its official website:
http://bit.ly/PhoebeParis

She then took a train through a tunnel under the English Channel and got to see England. It was a strange sight to see everyone driving on the opposite side of the road.

She read the signs and made her way to Buckingham Palace, and had tea and crumpets with the Queen!

The Queen was not amused and had her servants chase Phoebe away.

Join the Adventure!

Travel from Paris to London by train on this YouTube video: http://bit.ly/ParisTrain

Why do they drive on the left side of the road in England?

Would you be amused by a fly in your food?

What is the name of the Queen of England?

27

28

Phoebe noticed the royal helicopter was headed to Greece and hitched a ride.

Join the Adventure!

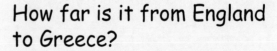

Who invented the helicopter?

With its long body and overhead wings, what insect does a helicopter look like?

How far is it from England to Greece?

What is the same about the countries of England and Greece?

In Greece, Phoebe saw the Acropolis and the original site of the first Olympics, high in the mountains with snow-capped peaks.

Join the Adventure!

To get to Greece from England, what direction did Phoebe fly?

How high can a fly fly?

How high is the Acropolis?

The first Olympic games were held in honor of Zeus, king of the gods. Can you name any of the other gods or goddesses of Greek mythology?

Eventually she left Greece and flew over to Spain.

She stopped in for desayuno with the King.

Join the Adventure!

To get to Spain from Greece, what direction did Phoebe fly?

What sea touches both Greece and Spain?

What is a peninsula?

What time is it where you live when the King of Spain has his breakfast at 7 in the morning?

What is the name of the capital city of Spain?

There were endless groves of olives and oranges all the way to the island of Gibraltar.

Join the Adventure!

What is similar about olives and oranges?

What is different about them?

Why do they grow so well in southern Spain?

What foods grow where you live?

Save the seeds from an orange and let them dry. Plant them all together in a pot of soil. What 3 things do the seeds need to sprout and grow into orange trees?

37

There were monkeys perched on cannons, high on the Rock of Gibraltar.

From up there, she could see Morocco, the country at the very northernmost edge of Africa.

Phoebe hitched a two hour ride on the ferry from Tarifa to Morocco.

Join the Adventure!

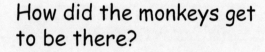

Why are there cannons on the Rock of Gibraltar?

How did the monkeys get to be there?

To see the monkeys of Gibraltar:
http://bit.ly/PhoebeMonkeys

Why didn't Phoebe take a train?

Is Morocco north or south of the Equator? Is Morocco more north or south than where you live?

It was well worth the journey!

The meat market in Marrakesh was unforgettable.

It was heaven on earth for a fly.

Join the Adventure!

Muslim women wear different kinds of coverings over their clothes. They are called different things, such as hijab, niqab, burka. Learn about these and more at http://bit.ly/MuslimWear

Why would Phoebe find the meat market to be unforgettable?

If there was a genie in the green bottle, where would you wish to go?

Would you prefer a monkey or a cat for a pet? Why?

What language is spoken in Marrakesh?

40

41

By now, Phoebe had mastered trains, buses, taxis, and planes.

She made her way to Australia, and chased kangaroos on the back of a dingo.

Join the Adventure!

Does Phoebe fly or ride more?

Is Australia an island like England?

Why would a dingo chase a kangaroo?

A kangaroo is a marsupial. Are there marsupials in America?

Learn lots about dingos on Animal Planet's website here: http://bit.ly/PhoebeDingos

Would it be wise to have a dingo as a pet?

She made it to Easter Island and saw the huge stone heads carved out of volcanic rock.

It was a strange place indeed. There were no bunnies in sight and chocolate was hard to find.

Join the Adventure!

In which ocean is Easter Island?

What direction did Phoebe fly to get there?

What volcano is closest to you? How could you travel there?

Why is Phoebe looking for bunnies and chocolate?

Enjoy a virtual visit and see the heads for yourself. Go to http://www.googlemaps.com then type into the search box: Easter Island. Drag the little gold guy to the green dots.

She went to South America and spent the night in a condor's nest.

At least she thought it was a condor. She wasn't an ornithologist.

Join the Adventure!

The condors are one of the largest birds in the world that can fly. Why do they live only where there are strong winds?

Learn about Andean Condors here at National Geographic's website: http://on.natgeo.com/1UL3LqQ

Besides the fact that they both fly, why is Phoebe like a condor?

What birds live where you live? Which one is the biggest? Which one is the smallest? Which one is the prettiest?

She tasted fried piranha on the banks of the mighty Amazon River.

Join the Adventure!

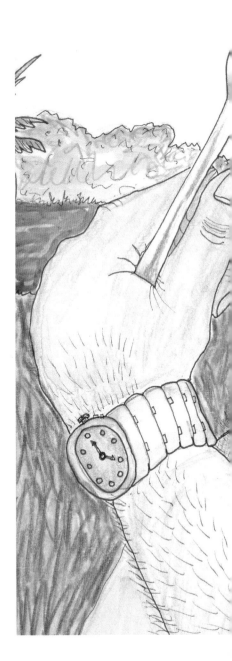

Piranha are carnivores. They eat meat, but they will eat anything that falls into their waters. An animal that eats only plants is called an herbivore. An animal that eats all sorts of things is called an omnivore. Which are you?

Learn more about piranha at http://bit.ly/piranahs

The Amazon carries more water than any other river in the world. What river is close to you?

Words which have more than one meaning are called homonyms. Are these "banks" for money or dirt?

47

She braved the blistering sun of Egypt and saw the Pyramids and the Sphinx.

Join the Adventure!

Where did you have to be brave to go?

How many sides does a pyramid have?

What is a sphinx?

On what continent is Egypt?

The Nile River flows right by the Pyramids. Is it as long as the Amazon?

Ask your smart phone or search the internet to find out the temperature today in Cairo, Egypt. Is your home hotter or cooler?

Enjoy a virtual visit to the Pyramids. Go to http://www.googlemaps.com then type into the search box: Great Pyramid of Giza

She traveled to the North Pole, but never got off the plane.

Phoebe decided it was far too cold for a fly. And besides, there were Polar Bears everywhere!

Join the Adventure!

Why doesn't this plane have wheels?

What temperature makes a fly not fly?

At what temperature does water freeze?

Is it ever NOT freezing at the North Pole?

Like puzzles? Have fun with these two virtual Polar Bear jigsaw puzzles:

http://bit.ly/BearPuzzle1 and http://bit.ly/BearPuzzle2

52

In her travels Phoebe had seen the Atlantic Ocean, the Pacific Ocean, the Indian Ocean, and the Arctic Ocean.

She had seen the Red Sea, the Dead Sea, the Yellow Sea, the Black Sea, and the Adriatic Sea, but they all seemed some shade of blue to her.

Phoebe had been gone almost a month, which, for a fly, is almost a lifetime.

She was homesick, and decided it was time to go home. She really missed her 150 brothers and sisters, and especially her mom and dad.

Join the Adventure!

Why is water blue?

Is the Red Sea red?

Is the Dead Sea dead?

What sea are you closest to?

In the next airport, Phoebe spotted a large man wearing a cowboy hat with a rattlesnake hat band. It smelled like barbeque.

She stayed on the hat all the way back to Houston. Even though they had a 6-hour layover and went through 3 different countries.

When the man pulled up in his driveway, Phoebe realized she was only two doors down from her very own house!

Join the Adventure!

How could Phoebe find an airport?

How did she know the man was going to Texas?

Why does a rattlesnake rattle?

How does a rattlesnake make sound? Go here to hear a rattlesnake: http://bit.ly/PhoebeSnake

55

56

She flew down the street as fast as she could.

Join the Adventure!

If Phoebe flew about 8 kilometers per hour, how many miles per hour did she fly?

If a male horsefly can fly at 90 miles an hour, how many times faster is that than Phoebe's flight?

Learn lots more about the flight of flies at the National Geographic website here: http://bit.ly/PhoebeFlies

Her mom and dad were there waiting by the green trash can.

At first they were angry because they were so worried about Phoebe, being the smallest and all. She hadn't called or written once!

After Phoebe explained where she had been, and all the things she'd seen, they were both really proud of her.

Her dad even said that Phoebe had probably flown further than any fly had ever flown!

Her mom was excited that Phoebe could say "Good Morning" in 5 different languages.

In that moment Phoebe felt a little taller.

Join the Adventure!

Why didn't Phoebe call?

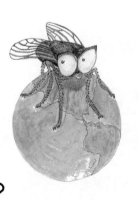

Are you the smallest?

What makes you feel taller?

Then Phoebe realized that despite all her travels and adventures, and the many new flies and interesting people she had met and all the amazing places she had seen, she didn't have any souvenirs or gifts.

The coins were far too heavy and a camera was out of the question.

Her mom said, "In the end, all you have is memories."

Join the Adventure!

Why didn't she bring home any souvenirs or gifts?

What is the smallest coin in American money? How much does it weigh?

What did Phoebe's mom mean when she said, "In the end, all you have is memories."? Do you have memories of a trip you have taken? Do you have souvenirs too?

62

Phoebe felt so good to be home again.

When she was younger, she was always trying to figure out how to leave. Now she realized that it was those same things that made her want to stay.

There was one thing she knew in her heart: There is no place she would rather be than home!

Join the Adventure!

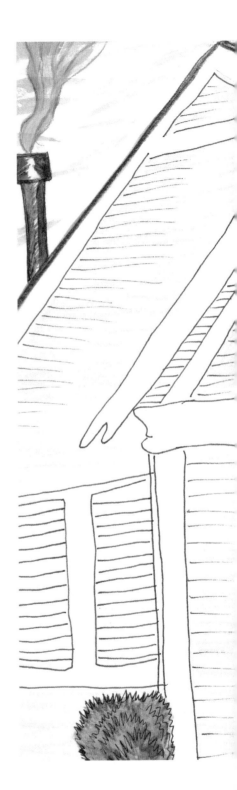

Where is the farthest place you have visited?

How long did it take you to get to that place?

What was your favorite thing about that place?

What are your favorite things about your home?

What do you know, deep in your heart?

64

Glossary & Pronunciation Guide

Acropolis: Uh-KROP-us-lus, the highest place in a city, built for military defense; in Ancient Greece, the Parthenon was at the Acropolis

Adriatic: AY-dree-yat-ic, body of water between Italy's boot and Eastern Europe

advantage: benefit, something good

amused: uh-MYUZD, entertained

banks: high pile of something

barbeque: food cooked over an outdoor fire

braved: was adventurous and bold

Buckingham Palace: the Queen's home in London

carnivore: CAR-nuh-vor, meat eater

carrier: box that makes something easy to carry

catalog: book that contains many things

caviar: CAV-ee-AR, salt-cured fish eggs, or roe, traditionally from wild sturgeon, but also salmon, trout, and other fish

condor: a type of vulture from the Americas which has a very large wingspan

continent: one of the Earth's seven major areas of land

crumpets: a thin muffin-like pancake

Customs: the department of a government that protects the country's borders

DaVinci: duh-VINN-chee, an Italian painter, sculptor, musician, engineer, and scientist

demonstration: showing of how to do something

desayuno: des-ah-YU-no, Spanish word for breakfast

dingo: wild dog in Australia

dumpster: large metal trash container

Egypt: EE-jipt, northeastern African country

Eiffel Tower: I-fuhl TOW-er, 984-foot iron tower in Paris

environment: everything around you any place where you are

eventually: at last, finally

extraordinary: beyond regular or every day

ferry: boat or ship that takes people and things across the water

flight attendant: man or woman who helps people when they fly

Gibraltar: jib-RAWL-ter, a British crown colony with a fort and port on a narrow finger of land at the southern tip of Spain

Giza: GEE-zuh, third largest city in Egypt where the pyramids were built

groves: groups of trees

Harvard University: in Massachusetts, Harvard is one of the oldest in America

herbivore: ER-biv-or, plant eater

homesick: sad longing for one's home

homonyms: words that sounds the same and are spelled the same but have different meanings

hydraulics: HI-draw-lix, science of using liquid with machines to move things

inspiration: an idea that makes you do things

investigate: explore

journey: trip

kilometer: kill-AH-muht-er, 1,000 meters or a bit more than half a mile

knack: NAK, talent

layover: wait between parts of a trip

Louvre: LU-vruh, museum in Paris

Marrakesh: MAR-uh-kesh, city in northern Morocco

Morocco: mor-AHK-ko, country at the northern tip of Africa, just across from Spain

Muslim: MUHZ-lihm, person who follows the religion of Islam

National Geographic: NASH-uh-null jee-uh-GRAFF-ik, large group of people who study the earth's surface, make maps, and explore

Olympics: games for people from all over the world who are not professionals

omelet: AHM-leht, scrambled eggs made into a flat shape then folded over with meat and vegetables

omnivore: AHM-nuh-VOR, eats everything

ornithologist: OR-nuh-THOLL-uh-jist, scientist who studies birds

paragraph: PAR-uh-graff, more than one sentence written to develop a certain idea

Phoebe Phyllis McGillicutty: FEE-bee FILL-us muh-GILL-uh-cuhddee

Picasso: pee-KOSS-so, Spanish painter and sculptor

piranha: PUH-rah-nuh, a small fresh water fish from South America that eats much larger animals

proliferation: pro-LIFF-er-AY-shun, fast growth

Pyramid: PEER-uh-mid, a structure with triangle sides and a square bottom

rattlesnake: a poisonous snake with a warning rattle at the tip of its tail

rumbling: a long, low, rolling sound

Santa Fe: SAN-tuh FAY, town in southeast Texas, near Houston

siblings: brothers and/or sisters

souvenir: reminder of a place, time or event

Sphinx: SFEENX, giant Egyptian statue of a lion with man's head

Tarifa: tah-REE-fuh, city in southern Spain, just across from Tangier

taxis: TAX-eez, more than one cab

tease: to make fun of, can be in a mean way

volcanic: vol-CAN-ik, something that comes from from a mountain made of melted rock

wondrous: WUN-druss, something that is amazing and wonderful

Phoebe's Fabulous Journey

1. Santa Fe, Texas >> START

2. Paris, France >> 5,030 miles

3. London, England >> 213 miles

4. Acropolis, Greece >> 1,985 miles

5. Madrid, Spain >> 2,296 miles

6. Gibraltar, Spain >> 409 miles

7. Tarifa, Spain >> 27 miles

8. Marrakesh, Morocco >> 336 miles

9. Alice Springs, Australia >> 9,894 miles

10. Easter Island >> 6,946 miles

11. Santiago, South America >> 2,334 miles

12. Manaus, South America >> 3,107 miles

13. Giza, Egypt >> 6,393 miles

14. North Pole >> 4,150 miles

15. Houston, Texas >> 4,167 miles >> HOME!

Use a spreadsheet to calculate how many miles Phoebe flew in all.

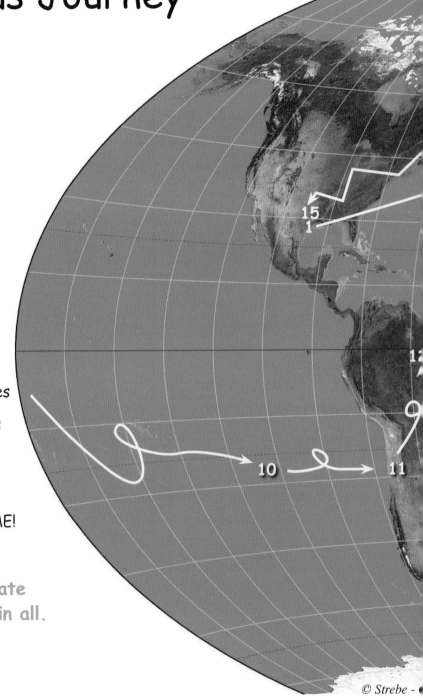

© Strebe -

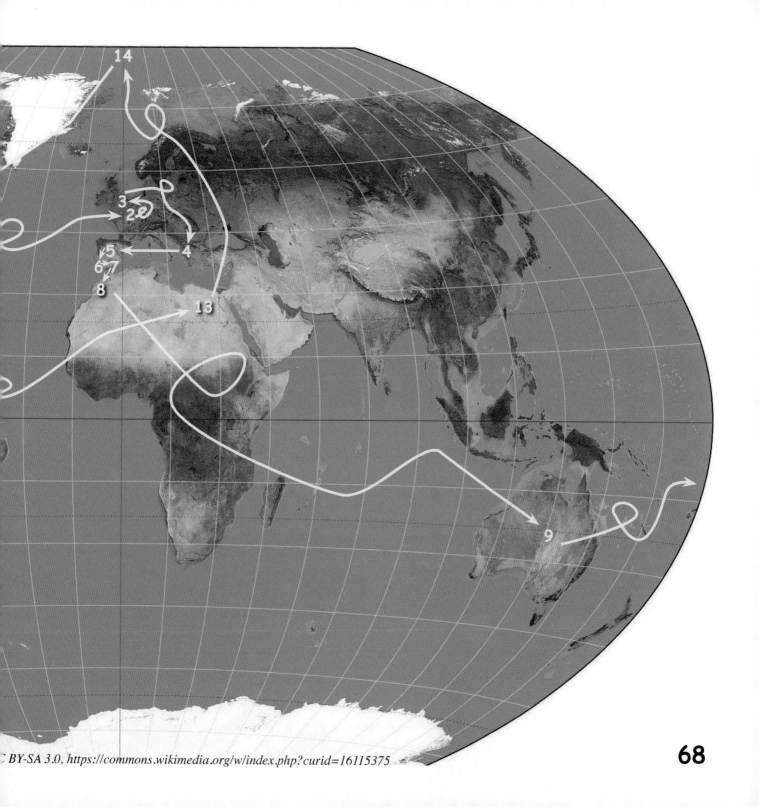

Phoebe's Fun Facts & Phenomena

Garbage Trucks

The Dempster-Dumpster was invented by George Dempster in 1935. He created the heavy equipment to do the work of many people in a short time. To learn more about the history of the Dumpster and garbage trucks, go to http://bit.ly/PhoebeDumpster

ClassicRefuseTrucks.com

Maggots

When fly eggs hatch the babies are called maggots. While they are wormy and squiggly and kind of gross, they are also very helpful. Phoebe's family, and all flies, actually recycle. They eat

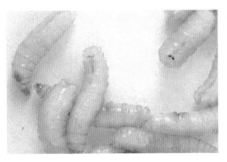

things that smell bad and are rotting, and turn them into dirt, much like worms. Without Phoebe and her siblings doing the dirty work for us, there would be lots of really nasty things in our world. Like the garbage men, maggots take out the stuff that you don't want or need any more.

Maggots have been used in medicine for many years. Though antibiotics have been used to do their job, sometimes medicine can't work like Nature can. Much like leeches help take out blood **69** from swollen wounds, maggots take out the dying flesh from places where people are hurt.

Venus Fly Traps

Yes, there are plants that eat meat. The Venus Fly Trap will eat anything it can get its little chompers on.

For a fun video of a Venus Fly Trap, go here: http://bit.ly/FlyTrapFun

You can buy a Venus Fly Trap plant and grow it at home. Just be sure to take good care of it.

Pocket Pals

Baby kangaroos are called joeys. They are very, very tiny when they are born. Too small to make it out in the world. At their birth, they crawl across their mama's fur and into her pocket. This is part of the mother's body and it has her nipples inside for the baby to get the milk it needs to grow.

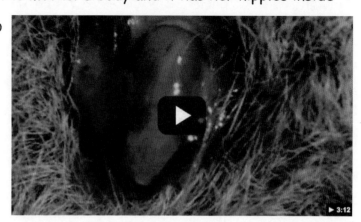

To see a baby kangaroo's birth and learn more about life for a joey, watch this National Geographic video: http://bit.ly/JoeyBirth

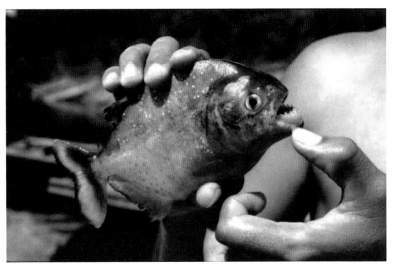

Piranah

These little fresh water fish from South America will eat anything they can get their little chompers on too. Their teeth are razor sharp. When an animal falls into their river, the school of fish enjoy a feast! If you go to South America, don't swim in the river.

Passport

Although Phoebe is just too small to carry a passport, you can create your very own! Copy the art shown here on the cover. On the inside, add the following to identify yourself: a photo of just your head, looking straight at the camera, home address, all parent name(s), phone number, and email address.

Then create a page for every country you visit in your studies. Identify the name of the country, which city you visited, how long you stayed, where you stayed, and why you went. Include photos of places you explored or visited. Write a one sentence review of each place to say why you would or would not return.

PASSPORT

UNITED STATES
OF
AMERICA

The Love of Languages

English	French	Greek	Spanish	Arabic
Hello	Bonjour >> bon-ZHUR	Χαίρετε >> HYER-et-tay	Hola >> OH-la	هتاف للترحيب >> MAHR-hab-bin
Good morning	Bonjour >> bon-ZHUR (Same as Hello)	Καλημέρα >> KAH-lee-meh-rah	Buenos días >> BWAY-nos DEE-yahs	باح جميل >> suh-BAH ahl-KHIR
Please	S'il vous plaît >> SEE-vu-play	παρακαλώ >> PAH-rah-kah-lo	Por favor >> POR fuh-VOR	من فضلك >> men-FAHD-lik
Thank you	Merci >> MAHR-see	ευχαριστώ >> EFF-HER-ee-stoe	Gracias >> GRAH-see-us	شكرا >> shook-RUN
Good-bye	Au Revoir >> aw-RIH-vwah	αντίο >> AD-nee-oh	Adiós >> AHD-yos	وداعا >> wuh-DAH-an

Add three words of your own and add how to write and say them in these other languages.

Not The End...